# SCHOOL MUSICAL

## STORIES FROM EAST HIGH #2

# WILDCAT SPIRIT

By Catherine Hapka

Based on the Disney Channel Original Movie
"High School Musical", written by Peter Barsocchini

Disney
PRESS

New York

Printed in the United States of America

First Edition
5 7 9 10 8 6 4

Library of Congress Catalog Card Number:2006935798
ISBN-13: 978-1-4231-0612-8
ISBN-10: 1-4231-0612-1

For more Disney Press fun, visit www.disneybooks.com
Visit DisneyChannel.com

# CHAPTER ONE

"**G**o, Wildcats!" Troy Bolton shouted as the basketball left his fingertips. A second later it swished through the basket—nothing but net.

He grinned as his teammates cheered. Troy's best friend, Chad Danforth, raced in and grabbed the ball, then sprang up and dunked it.

"That's what I'm talkin' about!" Chad crowed, doing a little victory dance under the basket.

Meanwhile, a couple of other teammates,

Zeke Baylor and Jason Cross, jogged over to give Troy a high five. "We are so ready for the game next Saturday," Zeke said. "We're going to totally slay Central!"

A whistle blew, echoing through the gym. "That's enough for today, guys." Coach Bolton, who was also Troy's father, surveyed his team proudly. "Have a great weekend and don't forget that East High's Spirit Week starts on Monday. I expect you guys to lead the way. Nobody has more school spirit than this Wildcats team!" His serious face cracked into a smile as the team cheered, and he winked. "I also expect to see one of you guys up there reigning as Spirit King at the big dance on Saturday night."

"Gee, I wonder who's going to win that title?" Chad said loudly, putting one finger to his chin and pretending to think hard.

The rest of the guys laughed. Zeke started the chant, and the others picked up on it—"Troy! Troy! *Troy!* TROYTROYTROY!" Chad pumped his fist in the air as he shouted along.

Coach Bolton grinned and strode off toward his office. Troy gave Chad a shove, making him drop the basketball tucked under his arm.

"Quit it, bro," Troy said. "If anybody should win that Spirit King title, it's Jason. He's the one who sank the three-pointer that won us the game last week."

"Nice try, Mr. Modesty." Chad scurried after the ball, which was bouncing across the floor.

"Yeah, give it up, Troy," Jason said. "Who could possibly have more school spirit than our superstar team captain? Everyone knows that title is yours—the only question is who's going to be your queen."

Zeke nodded. "Dude, you could show up wearing a hat on Pajamas Day and pajamas on School Colors Day, and you'd still win it in a walk. Nobody can touch you, man!"

"Dad always tells me, don't count your baskets until the points are on the board," Troy said, glancing in the direction in which his father had just gone. "So I'm not counting on anything."

"My man Troy does have a point," Jason said. "Don't forget, the teachers are the ones who make the decision. And who knows how they think? They could decide to give the title to one of their pet science nerds or something."

"No way!" Zeke shuddered, looking horrified. "A science nerd as Spirit King? That's just wrong."

"Yeah," one of the other guys muttered. "But it's possible."

"Whatever." Chad dribbled and shot, sending the basketball bouncing off the rim. "I just remembered, I need to hit the mall this weekend and buy some new pj's. My mom said if I leave the house in any of mine, she'll disown me and go into the Witness Protection Program."

Troy laughed. He'd seen Chad's closet, and he couldn't blame his mom. Every pair of pajamas Chad owned had huge holes in the knees; he was sometimes a little *too* enthusiastic when he playcd sock basketball in his room. The guy was obsessed. But that was one of the reasons Troy

4

liked him—he was obsessed with basketball, too.

"I still can't believe they want us to wear our pajamas to school," Jason commented as the team headed toward the locker room.

"Yeah, but think about how comfortable we'll be," one of the other guys said.

"I just hope I can stay awake during physics class," said Zeke.

As the guys continued to discuss the pros and cons of wearing pajamas to school, Troy was thinking about something else. He leaned back against the wall. "Maybe I need to hit the mall, too," he said, mostly to himself. "I want to get something cool to wear next Saturday night."

Chad sidled up to him, dribbling from hand to hand between his legs. "Sounds like someone's already thinking about the Spirit Ball," he said with a smirk. "So when are you going to ask her?"

Troy could feel his cheeks going as red as his Wildcats gym shorts. "I don't know what you're talking about," he mumbled.

But he knew *exactly* what Chad was talking about—Gabriella Montez. Ever since Troy had met Gabriella, she seemed to be all he could think about. She was smart, gorgeous, funny, and sweet. He'd never met a girl like her. Even the thought of going to a school dance with her on his arm, swaying to the music and holding her close, made him shiver. All he had to do now was figure out the perfect way to ask her. But what could that be?

"... so he can't ask her," Jason was saying.

"Huh?" Troy blinked, his fantasies dissolving instantly. "What did you just say?"

"Yo, Jason's right," Zeke put in, reaching out and stealing the ball from Chad. "You can't ask her, dude. It's a Sadie Hawkins dance."

"A whosie whatzit?" Chad asked, wrinkling his nose.

"Sadie Hawkins," Zeke explained. He bounced the ball against the wall in time with his words. "That means the girls have to ask the guys, not the other way around."

Now that he mentioned it, Troy remembered hearing something about that at the last school assembly. Somehow, it hadn't really sunk in until right now. "Oh, right," he murmured.

Chad was scratching his head through his mop of curly hair. "Who the heck is this Sadie Hawkins, and why is she messing with our dance?"

"I don't know," Jason told him. "But it means you won't be able to beg every girl in school to go with you, Danforth."

One of the other guys laughed. "Uh-oh, looks like Chad'll be going stag!"

"No way!" Chad exclaimed. "The ladies will be beating down my door. I'll just have to decide which one to grace with my studly presence."

Troy smiled as the rest of the team continued giving Chad a hard time. *So what if it's a Sadie Hawkins dance?* he asked himself. *No big deal. Actually, it makes my life easier. All I have to do is sit back and wait for an invite from Gabriella. . . .*

* * *

At that very moment, Gabriella was gathering up her things after the latest Scholastic Decathlon meeting. "See you all next week," she said with a smile. "Don't forget your school spirit!"

One of the other girls groaned. "I almost forgot," she said. "It'll be a whole week of rah-rah type sports stuff . . ."

". . . and silly pep rallies and dressing up like dorks . . ." said Martha, another team member.

". . . and the basketball team acting like Neanderthals," finished a skinny boy with glasses, named Timothy. "Even more than usual, I mean."

"Come on, it could be fun!" Gabriella said, laughing at their sour faces.

Her best friend, Taylor, pursed her lips. "Easy for you to say," she said. "You're just looking forward to going to that Spirit Ball next weekend with Troy."

Gabriella blushed. "That's not the only

reason," she protested. "I think the whole thing will be fun. I've never been part of a school Spirit Week before."

"Really?" Martha looked surprised.

"Really." Gabriella felt a twinge of sadness as she thought about all the schools she'd attended in her life. And thanks to her mother's job, she'd attended a *lot* of them before ending up at East High at the beginning of the winter semester.

But that's all over now, she reminded herself. Mom promised we won't move again until after I graduate.

The others were moving toward the classroom door, still discussing Spirit Week. Gabriella grabbed her bag and hurried to join them.

"Want to go shopping on Sunday?" she asked Taylor. "I want to look for something to wear to the dance."

"Sure." Taylor smiled. "But don't worry—Troy will think you look gorgeous no matter what you wear."

The others overheard. "So when are you going

to ask him, Gabriella?" Martha asked eagerly.

"Ask him?" Gabriella echoed. "What do you mean? Call me a traditionalist, but I was sort of hoping *he* would be the one to ask *me*. . . ."

Taylor shook her head. "Not this time," she said. "Sadie Hawkins dance, remember?"

"Really? Are you sure?" Gabriella stopped short in the doorway and turned to stare at her friend. "I don't remember hearing that."

"That's because you were too busy giggling at everything Troy said during the last assembly," Taylor said. "Principal Matsui mentioned the Sadie Hawkins thing at least three times."

"Oh." Gabriella gulped, staring out into the hallway. She'd never asked a boy out before. "Um, okay. I guess I have to ask him, then. Better to get it over with as soon as poss—" She let her voice trail off as she spotted Sharpay Evans walking by with her brother, Ryan. Or, more accurately, *flouncing* by. Sharpay never did anything as ordinary as *walking*.

"Hello, girls and boys," Sharpay said, striking

a dramatic pose as she leaned against a pillar. "Talking about the Spirit Ball?"

"That's what it sounded like to me," Ryan spoke up, nodding at what his sister had just said. He might have helped the other kids during the Battle of the Bands, but his true loyalty was still with Sharpay. Basically, if she said, "Jump," he'd ask, "How high?"

Not bothering to wait for anyone else to say anything, Sharpay stared down her nose at Gabriella. "Do my little ears deceive me, or did I just hear you say you're planning to ask Troy to be your date?"

"Of course she is," Taylor said. "Who else would she ask?"

Sharpay completely ignored Taylor. Her eyes were trained on Gabriella's face like a pair of charcoal-lined, mascaraed laser beams. Gabriella stared back, feeling vaguely nervous. Sharpay and Ryan had been the stars of every school musical except the last one—Gabriella and Troy had beaten them out for the lead roles that time. Gabriella was pretty sure Sharpay still hadn't quite forgotten that—or forgiven them for it.

"Well, if you want *my* advice . . ." Sharpay began.

"Um, actually, I don't remember hearing her ask for it," Taylor said.

Once again, Sharpay ignored her. "If you want my advice, you'll play it cool," she told Gabriella.

Ryan nodded wisely. "Sound advice."

"Play it cool? What do you mean?" Gabriella asked.

Sharpay shrugged, tossing her blond hair behind her shoulder with a practiced flick of her chin. "This is Troy Bolton we're talking about here," she said.

Yeah, Gabriella thought. Thanks for the news bulletin.

But Sharpay wasn't finished. "If you want a boy like Troy to take you seriously, you'd better not look too eager. *If* you know what I mean."

Gabriella wasn't entirely sure she did. But at

that moment, she heard her cell phone ring inside her bag. "Excuse me," she said, wondering if it was Troy calling. He should be getting out of basketball practice around now. . . . "Hello?" she said into the phone.

Her mother's voice answered, sounding tired and distracted. "Hey, sweetie, it's me. It looks like I'm going to be late for dinner tonight."

"Again?" Gabriella said with a sigh. "That's the third time this week! Doesn't your company know you have a life?"

"Sorry. No lives allowed." Her mother laughed, but she still sounded distracted. "See you later, okay?"

Gabriella said good-bye and hung up. "Everything okay?" Taylor asked her.

"Just Mom working too hard again. But what else is new?" Gabriella shrugged.

Taylor laughed. "Overachieving runs in the family, huh?"

Just then there was a shrill shriek of laughter from Sharpay. "What's so funny?" Gabriella asked, tucking her phone back into her bag.

"Your little brainiac friends here just asked who I thought would win Spirit King and Queen," Sharpay replied. She patted her hair. "Stupid question from such a smart bunch, don't you think? I would have thought that the queen, at least, was obvious. Toodles, children!" She started off down the hall with Ryan hurrying along at her heels. Then she paused and glanced back over her shoulder. "Remember what I said, Gabriella," she added. "You don't want to look too eager, am I right?"

"Sure," Gabriella said. Sometimes it was easier just to follow Ryan's lead and agree with whatever Sharpay said.

# CHAPTER TWO

"Check it out." Chad elbowed Troy in the ribs. "There's your girlfriend."

Troy looked where Chad was staring. Sure enough, Gabriella was sitting across the food court with Taylor and Martha and a few other friends.

"Come on," Troy said. "Let's go say hi." He called to Zeke and Jason, who were browsing the sale racks in front of the nearby CD store. As the four of them made their way across the crowded food court, Troy couldn't take his eyes off Gabriella, who was sipping a soda and listening to the other girls talk.

Too bad we missed each other after practice on Friday, Troy thought. And then she was away at her Scholastic-competition thingy all day yesterday. But this is the perfect chance for her to ask me to the dance.

Gabriella spotted Troy when he was still a few tables away. Seeing him always made her smile, and today was no exception. He looked amazing in his Wildcats team jacket and faded jeans.

"Look," she said. "Here come the guys."

"Perfect." Taylor sat up a little straighter. "I was planning to ask Chad to the dance on Monday. But I might as well do it now and be ahead of schedule."

Gabriella ducked her head to hide a smile. Taylor was a very practical person. It shouldn't be a surprise that she would treat asking a boy for a date like . . . well, like some kind of chemistry equation to be solved as quickly as possible.

Soon the boys reached the table. "Hey, wassup?" Chad said, reaching for one of Taylor's French fries without bothering to ask.

"Hi," Troy added, with a warm smile just for Gabriella.

She smiled back. "Hi," she said.

Meanwhile Taylor pointed one finger at Chad. "I'm glad you're here," she said briskly. "Chad, will you be my date for the Spirit Ball next Saturday?"

Jason and Zeke immediately started whooping and whistling. "Whoa, check out the ladies' man!" Jason crowed, slapping Chad on the back so hard that he almost pushed him into the plate of French fries.

"Yeah," Zeke added. "Guess you weren't just fronting when you said the girls would be falling at your feet. Who knew you'd be the first guy on the team with a date?"

Chad's cheeks were turning red. "Uh, um . . ."

Gabriella traded an amused smile with Troy. It wasn't often that Chad Danforth was rendered speechless!

"Well?" Taylor said, sounding impatient.

Chad shrugged as his buddies continued to hoot and holler. "Thanks for the offer, babe," he said with a goofy grin. "I'll check my book and get back to you, okay?"

Taylor frowned. "What's that supposed to mean?" she demanded. "Will you go with me, or not?"

Chad held up both hands in front of him. "Whoa, what's with the pressure?" he exclaimed. "I just told you I'd let you know."

"Yeah, chill out," Jason said. "He has to make sure he doesn't already have a date with a super-model that night."

Zeke had just swiped one of Taylor's French fries. He laughed so hard that it almost flew out of his mouth. "Good one, bro!" he said, trading a high five with Jason.

"Shut up, dude." Chad punched him on the arm. "You're not helping."

As the other three guys shoved one another around, Troy slid into the empty chair beside

Gabriella. "So—speaking of the big dance . . . it should be fun, huh?" he said.

"Yeah. Fun." Gabriella barely heard him. She was too busy fuming over Chad's behavior toward Taylor. How could he act like such a jerk? Everyone knew he and Taylor liked each other. Although at the moment she wasn't sure what Taylor saw in him. . . .

Troy cleared his throat and leaned a little closer. "It's pretty cool how they made it a Susie Hawkins dance, isn't it?"

"It's *Sadie* Hawkins," Gabriella corrected automatically. But once again, she wasn't really paying full attention to Troy. She was sure that Taylor was feeling hurt by the way Chad was acting. And Chad was so busy clowning around with Zeke and Jason that he didn't even seem to notice.

Why are guys such jerks sometimes? Gabriella wondered. It's like they don't even notice that other people have feelings.

"So anyway . . ." Troy began.

Gabriella never even got the chance to hear

what Troy was about to say. At that moment, Taylor stood up and stormed off.

"Taylor, wait!" Gabriella cried. Leaving her soda on the table, she raced after her friend.

Fifteen minutes later, Troy was still thinking about Gabriella. Why hadn't she asked him to the dance? He'd certainly given her enough of an opening.

He wandered through the mall with the other guys, but he wasn't paying attention to the stores they were passing. When they reached their favorite sporting goods store, Jason had to ask Troy three times if he wanted to go inside.

"Sorry," Troy said, shaking his head to clear it of all thoughts of Gabriella. "Guess I'm a little out of it."

"Thinking about the big game next weekend?" Zeke asked.

"Nah, he's probably deciding which pajamas to wear to school tomorrow," Jason guessed.

Chad rolled his eyes. "Get a clue, dorks," he

said. "He's thinking about what he's always thinking about these days. I'll give you a hint— her initials are GM. And I'm *not* talking about the car company."

"You caught me this time," Troy admitted with a rueful smile. "It just doesn't make sense. Taylor asked you. Why didn't Gabriella ask me?"

Chad shrugged and poked at a pair of cleats on the sale rack outside the sports store. "Why do girls do anything, man?" he said. "Maybe she found another guy or something."

"Yeah, right." Troy knew that wasn't the problem. He just didn't know what the problem *was.* "Come on," he said, deciding not to think about it. "Let's go inside."

"Troy! Hey, Troy!"

Hearing his name as he entered the store, Troy turned to look. So did his friends.

"Yo, cheerleader alert," Jason said.

Sure enough, several members of East High's cheerleading squad were rushing toward them from the back of the store. In the lead was a perky, curly-haired cheerleader named Ami. She was waving and calling Troy's name.

"Hey, Ami," he greeted her when she reached him. "What's up?"

"I'm soooo glad I ran into you, Troy!" she cried, brushing a springy lock of hair out of her face. "Will you go to the dance with me?"

Troy was startled by the invitation. Somehow, it hadn't even occurred to him that anyone other than Gabriella would ask him. Didn't the whole school know by now that they were an item?

But Ami was gazing at him with a bright smile, waiting for an answer. "Um—uh—I'm sorry," he stammered, trying to ignore his friends, who were snorting and poking at each other as they watched. "I—I think I'm going with somebody else."

"Oh." Ami looked disappointed, but then she shrugged and turned to Jason with a smile. "How about you? Want to go with me?"

"Sure!" Jason said immediately. "I'm so there!"

"Cool!" Ami patted him on the arm. "It's a

date. See you at school tomorrow. I can't wait to see all you guys in your jammies!" She turned and hurried off with her friends, giggling.

Jason stared after her with a goofy look on his face. He touched the spot on his arm where she'd patted him. "Whoa," he said. "Sorry to swoop in like that, Troy. But you blew it, bro. She's totally hot!"

"Guess I did. Your gain, man." Troy shrugged and smiled. Sure, half the guys in school would kill to go to the dance with a girl like Ami. But not him. He was holding out for one very special girl.

Gabriella was lost in thought as she wandered up the front walkway of her house. She'd managed to convince Taylor that Chad was just kidding around in front of his basketball buddies. Of course he would say yes. Finally, Taylor had agreed to give him another chance to act like a human being and accept her invitation. Gabriella was relieved. But the whole incident had left a funny taste in her mouth.

I know Chad likes Taylor, she thought. So why would he act that way when she asked him out? It just doesn't make sense.

She chewed on her lower lip as she reached for the front door. A thought had just occurred to her. A very scary, weird thought: could Sharpay actually know what she was talking about?

"No way," Gabriella whispered.

She entered the front hallway and slung her shopping bags onto a chair. She could hear her mother's voice drifting toward her from the direction of the kitchen. It sounded like she was on the phone.

Gabriella headed down the hall. As she got closer, she realized her mother was using her business voice. She frowned. Could she really be taking a business call on Sunday afternoon?

She pushed open the kitchen door. Her mother was standing with her back to Gabriella, staring out the window over the sink as she talked.

"... and obviously, I can't just drop everything

and head off to New York next week," Mrs. Montez was saying into the phone. "We'll have to push back this move to next month at the earliest. Especially since I'll have to make arrangements with my daughter's school, and . . ."

Gabriella's eyes widened. Slapping one hand over her mouth to cover her gasp, she backed quickly out of the room before her mother could see her. Out in the hall, she leaned against the wall trying to make sense of what she'd just heard.

It sounded like her mother was talking about moving again!

# CHAPTER THREE

"Troy! Troy Bolton! Wait up!"

Troy had barely set foot inside East High on Monday morning when he saw Hannah, the cute, dark-haired girl from his algebra class running toward him. Well, maybe not *running* exactly—more like half running and half hopping. The fuzzy pink bedroom slippers she was wearing kept slipping off as she rushed across the school lobby. Today was Pajama Day, the first day of Spirit Week, and East High looked like a giant slumber party.

"What's up, Hannah?" Troy said, tugging at the shirt hem of his own plaid flannel pj's. It definitely felt weird to wear his pajamas to school. But it was kind of fun, too. "Ready for that algebra quiz today?"

"Yeah," Hannah said breathlessly. "I mean, no. I mean, who cares? I have something much more important to talk to you about. Will you go to the dance with me?"

Troy gulped. "Oh, wow," he said, stalling for time. Hannah was the fourth girl to ask him so far. There was Ami yesterday, and then two more girls had called last night. Not Gabriella, though . . . Even after all that practice saying no, Troy still wasn't sure what to say now that another girl was asking. "Um, I'm totally flattered. But I'm sort of planning to go with someone else."

"So I'm too late?" Hannah cried. "You already said yes to someone?"

"Sort of. Well, not really. I mean, I'm waiting for that to happen." Troy shrugged, feeling stupid. "That is, I'm expecting someone to ask me soon, but she hasn't quite yet. But I'm already sort of planning to, you know, say yes to her. So it's sort of like I already have, right?"

"Oh." Hannah looked crestfallen—and a little confused. "Okay."

"Excuse me!" They were both distracted by a loud voice coming from the direction of the front door. "Coming through."

Troy glanced over. His eyes widened as he saw Sharpay striding into the lobby. She was wearing a pair of bright red silk pajamas with little Wildcats logos printed all over them. On her feet, she wore leather slippers shaped like a pair of snarling wildcats. Spotting Troy, Sharpay waved and then marched right up to him, pushing Hannah out of her way.

"Pardon me, Heidi," Sharpay said. "I have something *tres* important to discuss with Troy." She shot the other girl a quick smile. For all her acting skills, Troy thought, it didn't look terribly convincing. "I'm sure you understand."

"My name is Hannah," Hannah said.

Sharpay had already turned toward Troy. At Hannah's response, she turned back and blinked at her. "Um, are you still here?" Without waiting for an answer, she spun again to smile at Troy. "Good morning, Troy. I love your pajamas."

Troy glanced at Hannah out of the corner of his eye as she rolled her eyes and stomped away, her fuzzy slippers slapping the tile floor. "I like yours, too, Sharpay," he said. "Very spirited."

"Thank you." Sharpay smoothed down her pajama top, looking pleased with herself. "I had them custom made. The slippers, too. Aren't they absolutely adorable?" She held up one foot so Troy could admire it.

Just then, Troy noticed a huge, fuzzy creature shuffling toward them. It was covered in beige fur and was wearing a Wildcats team tank top. Only a pair of grayish blue eyes showed that there was a human inside. And those eyes looked sort of familiar. . . .

"Ryan?" Troy said, peering past a shiny black rubber nose and a set of pipe-cleaner whiskers. "Is that you, man?"

"It's me," a miserable-sounding voice emerged from the mound of fur.

"Um . . . so is that really what you wear to sleep in?" Troy asked. Ryan could be a little eccentric. But this . . . ?

"Of course not," Sharpay answered for her brother. "He's part of my outfit. He's a stuffed Wildcat. Kind of like my own giant stuffed animal. It's Pajamas Day. Get it?"

Troy grinned. Leave it to Sharpay to go over the top, even on something as simple as Pajamas Day.

"O-o-okay," he said. "Lookin' good, man." He clapped Ryan on the shoulder.

Guess Sharpay's already angling for that Spirit Queen title, he thought. And we all know that when Sharpay wants something, she really goes for it!

"So, Troy," Sharpay said. "Do you have a date

for the Spirit Ball yet? Because it just so happens that I'm still—"

"Excuse me," Troy interrupted. He'd just spotted Gabriella walking in through the school doors. "I'll be right back, okay?"

"But I was just about to—"

Once again, he didn't let Sharpay finish her sentence. He took off toward Gabriella.

Gabriella was barely aware of the usual Monday-morning prehomeroom commotion all around her as she moved across the crowded lobby. She was thinking about what she'd overheard in the kitchen the afternoon before. In fact, she hadn't thought about much else since it happened. She'd almost forgotten it was Pajamas Day—luckily she'd remembered just in time, pulling on a pale blue nightgown and her favorite ballet-style slippers.

How could Mom even think about moving again? she asked herself for what had to be the fiftieth time. She promised she wouldn't do that to me. Not this time. This time, we were supposed to be here to stay.

"Gabriella!"

She snapped out of it when she realized Troy was hurrying toward her, waving and calling her name. Forcing a smile, she returned his wave.

"Nice pajamas," she said as he skidded to a stop in front of her.

"Thanks. Yours, too."

There was a moment of silence. Gabriella immediately drifted back to her earlier thoughts. Could it really be true? Could she be leaving East High so soon?

The trouble was, she still didn't know for sure. All she had to go on was that overheard phone call. Normally she had no trouble talking to her mother about anything. But this was different somehow. Maybe it was because she really didn't want to know the answer . . .

"Gabriella? Did you hear me?"

Once again, Gabriella snapped back to the here and now. "Sorry, Troy," she said. "Um, I guess it's kind of loud in here. What did you say?"

"I said, I wonder if Sharpay is going to bring a live wildcat as her date to the Spirit Ball to make sure she wins that Spirit Queen title." Troy laughed. "I can't wait to go to the dance and see, can you?"

"Um, sure. I mean, I can't wait either." Gabriella really didn't care what Sharpay did at that weekend's dance. She was much more concerned about whether she, herself, would ever get to attend another dance at East High. For a second she was tempted to share her worries with Troy. "Um, listen, Troy . . ."

But she stopped herself just in time, biting her tongue. What was she thinking?

"What is it?" Troy took a step closer, staring at her intently.

Gabriella shook her head. "Nothing." She couldn't believe she'd almost blurted out what she was thinking. Why ruin Troy's Spirit Week with such depressing news? "I mean, ah, I was just going to say I liked your slippers."

"Oh." Troy glanced down at his own feet

before meeting her eyes again. "Because for a second there, I thought you were going to—"

"Troy!" Sharpay came barging over, cutting him off in midsentence. "So *here's* where you disappeared to—didn't you promise you'd be right back?" She arranged her face into a playful pout. "And I *really* need to talk to you about something—in *private*."

For once, Gabriella didn't mind when Sharpay dragged Troy away. She was too distracted to talk to anybody at the moment, anyway. Even Troy.

I need to get a handle on this somehow, she thought. Otherwise my Spirit Week will be ruined—and my friends' week, too. And we should probably enjoy it as much as possible, considering it may be the last one we all have together.

She hurried out of the lobby and down the hall. On the way to her homeroom, she passed the school auditorium. The doors were open, and she heard the sounds of thumping and banging.

Gabriella paused and glanced inside. She immediately recognized Kelsi Nielsen, the composer of the winter musical. Kelsi was struggling to lift a large piece of red-and-black–striped plywood. As Gabriella watched, Kelsi finally got the piece of wood off the ground—and almost fell off the edge of the stage. At the last second, she let go of the wood, which went crashing to the floor.

"Are you okay?" Gabriella cried, hurrying toward her.

Kelsi jumped at Gabriella's words, almost falling off the stage again. "Oh! Hi, Gabriella," she said in her soft, shy voice. She shoved her wire-rimmed glasses back up her nose. "I didn't see you come in."

"What are you doing?" Gabriella glanced around the auditorium. It looked like it always did when the drama club was in the midst of a scenery-painting frenzy—sheets of plywood, paint cans, and other bits of equipment were littered everywhere. "Is there another musical coming up that I didn't hear about?"

Kelsi smiled and mopped a few beads of sweat from her forehead with the back of her hand. "Nothing like that," she said. "This is for the dance on Saturday. Ms. Darbus is in charge of decorating, and she wants the place to, um, glitter and pop like the set of the Tony awards."

Gabriella laughed. "That sounds like Ms. Darbus!" she said, thinking of the school's drama teacher. She also realized with a twinge of guilt that she hadn't asked Troy to the dance yet. . . . "And it also sounds like too big a job for one person. Need some help?"

"Thanks," Kelsi said gratefully. "Now that you mention it . . ."

Gabriella dropped her bag on a chair and hurried forward to grab one end of the plywood sheet. Kelsi wasn't the type of person to ask for help unless she was really desperate. She just stepped up and did what needed to be done. Gabriella figured the least she could do was help her out this time. Besides, Kelsi was good at keeping secrets. If Gabriella confided in her about what she'd overheard, maybe she could get some advice about her problem. . . .

# CHAPTER FOUR

"Check it out!" somebody cried in the crowded school lobby the next morning. "Sharpay has a house on her head!"

Troy glanced up from talking with his buddies just in time to see Sharpay marching proudly through the front door. His jaw dropped in amazement. She had an enormous contraption balanced precariously atop her head. It appeared to be some kind of mutant dollhouse that she had attached to a large hat.

"What *is* that thing?" somebody asked Sharpay loudly.

She stopped in the middle of the room and struck a pose. "Isn't it obvious?" she asked, her stage-trained voice carrying to every corner of the lobby. "It's my hat for Hat Day, of course! It's a scale model of our own beloved East High. See?" She lifted one hand and pointed carefully at something at the top of the structure on her head. "That's me on the roof, waving the school flag."

Troy ducked behind Zeke as Sharpay turned on her heels, the edifice atop her head wobbling as she glanced around. She seemed to be looking for someone, and he didn't want her to spot him. Sharpay had asked him to the dance twice the day before, including the time she'd dragged him away from Gabriella before homeroom. Troy definitely didn't want to have to find a new, even more creative way to turn her down yet again.

"Whoa," Chad said, still staring at Sharpay.

"Somebody should tell that girl today is *Hat* Day, not Pile-Everything-but-the-Kitchen-Sink-on-Your-Head Day."

Jason was grinning. "Good thing her neck is already used to carrying her big, swelled head around," he joked. "Otherwise, it would snap in two under all that weight."

Troy chuckled, but he wasn't paying that much attention. He had been keeping an eye out for Gabriella since arriving at school, and he'd just spotted her entering the lobby.

"Catch you later, guys," he told his teammates. Then he jogged over to Gabriella. "Hey!" he greeted her. "Nice hat."

Gabriella reached up and touched the brim of the plain blue baseball cap she was wearing. "Not really," she said with a laugh. "I almost forgot today was Hat Day. This was the best I could find on short notice."

"Really? In that case, here." Troy grabbed his own hat, a cool striped top hat. "We can swap."

"No, really. That's okay," Gabriella protested.

"I insist." Troy pushed his hat into her hands. "You don't want to look like a chump for the homeroom hat parade, do you?" He laughed. "Especially after the humiliation of watching Chad win that Best Pajamas award yesterday."

Gabriella grinned. Somehow, even when she was feeling down, Troy could make her feel at least a little bit better.

"Thanks," she said, making the trade. She put on his striped hat. It was a tad big, but it still felt good. "And don't worry—if I win that Hat award, I won't forget to thank you in my acceptance speech."

"Deal." Troy smiled at her and didn't say anything else. He just stood there with her baseball cap in his hands, waiting for her to say something else.

Gabriella cleared her throat nervously. She wondered if he could tell there was something up with her lately. Sharing her secret with Kelsi yesterday had made her feel better for a little while, but today her worries were back at full strength. I really haven't been acting like myself, she thought. I'm sure he can tell there's something bugging me this week.

"So . . ." Troy said after a long moment of silence. "Is there anything you—"

Before he could finish, the bell rang to call everyone to homeroom. "Oops, we'd better get moving," Gabriella said, relieved to be saved by the bell. She reached up to pat the hat on her head. "I don't want to waste this baby by missing that parade."

By the time the final bell rang, Troy was starting to wonder if he was living in a parallel universe— one where Gabriella Montez didn't have any intention of asking him to the Spirit Ball. Because no matter how many times he managed to run into her between classes and how many hints he dropped, she still hadn't said a word about it.

"She ask you yet, bro?" Chad asked him as they met up at their lockers before basketball practice.

Troy shook his head and sighed. "Nope," he said. "But Susan Kane did. So did Ashley Ramirez."

"What about Sharpay?" Chad asked.

Troy rolled his eyes. "Yeah, her, too," he said. "Three times."

"That girl doesn't know how to take no for an answer!" Chad laughed. "You should've heard her arguing with Ms. Darbus after she awarded Best Hat to Cyndra this morning. I'm telling you, Sharpay is wasted here in high school—she should be on the Supreme Court or something!"

Troy chuckled, but he wasn't all that amused. He was getting tired of saying no to other girls. What was Gabriella waiting for? When was she going to ask him? Or *was* she? He was really starting to wonder.

"Ready to hit the gym, bro?" Chad asked, slamming his locker shut. "Practice starts in twenty."

"I'll meet you there," Troy said.

He lingered by his locker for a while after

Chad left, then wandered down the hall looking for Gabriella. Despite his doubts, he wasn't ready to give up yet. Maybe she was just too shy to ask him out in front of other people. If he could just get her alone for a few minutes, maybe drop a few more subtle hints . . .

By the time Troy gave up on finding Gabriella, the halls of East High were silent and empty. Everybody had already left school or disappeared into their meetings, practices, and rehearsals. Troy put on a burst of speed as he neared the gym. He knew Principal Matsui would get on his case if he caught him running in the halls. But he was less worried about that than he was about what his father would say if he was late.

Luckily he made it into the gym just seconds before his dad blew the whistle to start practice. Chad nudged him.

"Where's Zeke?" he whispered. "Did you see him on your way in?"

Troy merely shook his head, shooting his dad a glance out of the corner of his eye. As he did, he saw Zeke come skidding into the gym, out of breath and covered with a white substance that looked suspiciously like flour.

Coach Bolton saw him, too. "Glad you could join us, Mr. Baylor," he said sarcastically.

"Sorry, Coach." Zeke panted, doing his best to brush himself off. "Lost track of time. Won't happen again."

"See that it doesn't."

Zeke jogged over and joined the other guys. "What's with you, man?" Jason whispered.

"The clock in the home-ec lab is slow," Zeke whispered back.

"The home-ec lab?" Chad rolled his eyes. "Man, you are spending *way* too much time in that place!"

Troy was surprised, too. It wasn't long ago that they'd all learned Zeke's secret—he loved to bake. In his spare time, he made all sorts of cakes, cookies, pies, and pastries—and his crème brûlée was already the stuff of legend. But being late for practice because he

45

was baking after school? That wasn't like him.

"So what's the deal?" Jason asked. "You planning to quit the Wildcats and start the East High pastry team?"

"Nothing like that." Zeke shook his head. "It's because of Spirit Week. I've been helping out, making cookies and stuff for the ball on Saturday. I just took a whole batch of Wildcat cookies out of the oven."

Troy's stomach grumbled. He'd been so busy talking to Gabriella and dropping hints about the dance at lunchtime that he'd barely eaten anything. A few of Zeke's cookies sounded good just about now. . . . "That's cool," he said, licking his lips. "Can't wait to taste one."

"Yeah, right. Won't be so cool if we lose the game 'cause Zeke's thinking harder about frosting than free throws," Chad put in. "You gotta keep your head in the game, man!"

"You don't have to worry about me," Zeke said quickly. "I'll be there, one hundred and fifty percent. Oh! But wait until you guys see the special cookies I'm designing for the Spirit King and Queen. They're shaped like little crowns—get it? For king and queen?" He grinned proudly, absentmindedly brushing flour off his arm. "It took me a while to figure out how to make them look like they were made out of gold, though." He elbowed Troy and winked. "I hope you like banana frosting, Your Majesty."

A sharp whistle interrupted them. "Hey!" Coach Bolton barked. "Enough talking. Are you boys on the Wildcats or the gossip squad?"

"Wildcats!" Jason, Chad, and Zeke yelled.

Troy pumped his fist. "Go, Wildcats!" he added.

"Good." His father looked satisfied. "Then let's start that new layup drill we did last time. Let me see you hustle!"

# CHAPTER FIVE

"**H**ey, Gabriella! Where's your twin?" someone yelled as Gabriella stepped off the school bus on Wednesday morning.

Gabriella smiled weakly at the girl who'd asked. "Only child here," she quipped. "No twin for me."

She hurried on toward the door before the girl could ask any more questions. The girl shrugged, turning to whisper something to the "twin" standing next to her. Both of them were dressed in jeans and pink sweaters, and they had matching scarves tied around their necks.

I'm *so* not in the mood for this, Gabriella thought, glancing around. Everywhere she looked, she saw double. It was Twin Day, and people were going all out, just as they had for Pajamas Day and Hat Day.

Gabriella knew it was her own fault that she looked out of place. Both Troy and Taylor had asked her to be their twin. But Gabriella had turned down both of them. She was too worried about the whole moving thing to think about something as silly as matching clothes.

Instead, she'd been spending every spare moment wondering how she could have been stupid enough to believe she was really at East High to stay. How many times had she been through this? True, those other times her mother hadn't made any promises. But still, hadn't she just been thinking about how hard her mother was working lately? Sort of the way she always did when she was preparing for another big promotion . . . ?

Anyway, Gabriella thought as she dodged several more sets of twins, if I'm going to be starting at another new school soon, I might as well get used to feeling like the odd one out. Because there's no way I'll ever feel at home at another school the way I do at this one . . .

At that same moment, Troy was wandering down the hall toward homeroom, feeling a little out of place in a school full of matching outfits. He broke into a smile when he spotted Chad loping toward him. He looked just like he did every day—dressed in jeans and a T-shirt, with a basketball tucked under one arm.

"Yo, there you are!" Troy exclaimed, hurrying over to trade high fives with his friend. "I was starting to think I was the only one in the entire school without a twin. Looks like you're on your own, too, huh? Want to change into our team shirts or something so we'll match up?"

"Sorry, bro." Chad shook his head. "I've already got a twin."

"You do? Who?" Troy asked in surprise. He knew Zeke and Jason had decided to pair up, and the rest of the team was spoken for, too.

"Taylor. I'm supposed to be meeting her by her locker right now—she brought a hat for me to wear or something."

Troy felt his heart sink. He'd tried to call Chad last night after Gabriella had said no to being his twin. But the line had been busy for over an hour, and finally he'd given up. Now he realized his friend must have been talking with Taylor.

"So does this mean you guys are cool again?" he asked. "Last I heard, she was still mad at you for acting like such a dork the other day at the mall."

Chad shrugged sheepishly. "She's still kind of mad," he said. "But since Gabriella didn't want to be her twin, she decided I would have to do." He spun his basketball on the tip of one finger. "I figure it'll give me the perfect chance to win her over again with my charm and wit."

Troy was glad to hear that the two of them

were on their way to making up after their fight. But this meant he really was on his own today.

"Oh, well," he said, trying not to sound too disappointed. "Looks like I'm just going to have to be the guy without a twin all day." He held up his hands as if framing a marquee title. "Sounds like a made-for-TV movie, doesn't it? *The Guy Without a Twin*."

"Yoo-hoo, Troy!" Sharpay rushed up to them. "Did I just hear you say you don't have a twin?"

Troy winced, wishing he'd kept his voice down. Chad grinned and faded away into the crowd. "That's right, Sharpay," Troy said. "I'm afraid I'm twinless. Looks like you and Ryan have your act together as usual, though."

Sharpay shot a glance at her brother, who was right behind her. Both of them were wearing black pants with rhinestones down the sides, silky white shirts, red bolero jackets, and jaunty red hats with black feathers. When Ryan turned for a second to brush a speck of lint off his pants, Troy saw that there was a Wildcats logo on the back of his jacket, outlined in black and silver glitter.

"Oh. Right." Sharpay shrugged, then turned to smile at Troy. "But I'm sure Ryan wouldn't mind if you took his place. After all, we can't have the captain of the basketball team and the future Spirit King of East High . . ." She paused just long enough to give an obvious wink and smirk. ". . . without a twin for Twin Day! That just wouldn't look right."

"Oh, I don't know . . ." Troy began.

Sharpay rested one hand on his arm, smiling up at him. "You don't have to thank me," she said. "It would be an honor to be your twin. In fact, it gives us a chance to practice looking good together—you know, for when we're crowned on Saturday night." She tapped her chin with one finger, which Troy noticed was manicured in matching red with black glitter. "Come to think of it, the whole spirit-royalty thing gives us all the more reason to go to the ball together. Want to reconsider?"

Troy opened his mouth to say no again, then hesitated. Was he making a fool of himself by waiting around for Gabriella to ask him to the dance? Maybe she wasn't planning to ask him at all. What would he do then? Aside from Sharpay, all the other girls who'd asked him had gone ahead and asked other guys. And he was going to look like the world's biggest loser if he was the only one on the team without a date.

But as far as he knew, Gabriella hadn't asked anyone else. That meant there was still hope. Didn't it?

He shook his head firmly, trying to ignore his doubts. "I already told you, Sharpay. I don't think that's a good idea."

"Really? Because a little birdie told me you still don't have a date. And if there's one thing worse than a Spirit King without a twin . . . Well, whatever." Sharpay flicked her fingers, as if shooing away a pesky fly. "Now, why don't you and Ryan go into the little boys' room and trade outfits?"

Ryan cleared his throat, looking anxious. "Wait—maybe we could all be triplets instead," he suggested. "I'm sure we could find Troy a matching outfit in the Drama Club costume closet."

"Triplets?" Sharpay rolled her eyes. "I think not. Didn't you ever hear the saying 'three's a crowd'?" She turned back toward Troy. "Now, Troy, about the dance . . ."

"Come on, Ryan," Troy said quickly. "Let's go switch outfits."

He wasn't exactly thrilled about walking around school looking like a matador who had fallen into a vat of glitter. But he decided it was a small price to pay to get Sharpay to shut up about the dance for a while. He needed to figure out what to do about Gabriella.

By the time Troy emerged from the men's room, he had come up with a plan.

It's like when we're two points behind with a minute to go, he thought, adjusting his hat so he could see past its droopy black feather. There's no more time to mess around. I need to grab the ball and make a drive for the basket—er, I mean find Gabriella and just come out and ask her if she's ever planning to ask me to that dance.

Having reached that decision, he already felt a little bit better. He was used to being a play-maker on the basketball team. Was this sort of situation really that different?

"See you later, dude," Troy told Ryan, who seemed a bit disgruntled as he stared down at the faded blue jeans and gray hoodie he was now wearing. "I need to, um, run an errand."

He took off without waiting for an answer, heading straight to Ms. Darbus's homeroom to see if Gabriella was there yet. She wasn't, though Taylor was, tapping her foot and staring at her watch.

"Troy!" she exclaimed when she spotted him. "Have you seen Chad?"

"Yeah, a few minutes ago," Troy said distract-edly as he glanced around the room. Only a few students were there this early. "He was going to meet you at your locker. Have you seen Gabriella?"

"At my locker?" Taylor cried, throwing both hands in the air. "What's wrong with that boy? I *told* him to meet me *here!*"

She stomped toward the door, brushing past Troy on her way. "Taylor!" he called urgently. "Gabriella—do you know where she is?"

"Oh!" Taylor paused, shooting him an apologetic smile. "Nope, sorry. Haven't seen her."

Troy sighed as Taylor disappeared through the classroom door. He turned and followed her out, rushing through the halls in search of Gabriella. She wasn't at her locker. There was no sign of her in the chemistry lab. And when he stuck his head into the auditorium, the only people in sight were Kelsi and Zeke.

"Hi, Troy!" Zeke waved a paintbrush at him. "Did you come to help us work on decorations for the dance? I told Kelsi I'd help her while my latest batch of cookies is cooling."

"Maybe later, okay?" Troy was so distracted that he barely took in what his teammate was saying. "Uh, Gabriella hasn't been here, has she?"

"Nope, not today," Kelsi replied, dipping her paintbrush into a bucket of red paint.

"Okay, thanks anyway. See you."

It was only when Troy found himself back in the lobby that he finally spotted Gabriella. She was standing with Ryan, laughing as he fiddled with something in her hair.

"Gabriella!" Troy cried.

Gabriella looked up when she heard Troy calling her name. Her laugh froze on her lips. He was dressed in some kind of ridiculous outfit that looked a couple of sizes too small for him. But even so, he still looked cute.

For a few minutes, Ryan had actually helped her forget about her problems. Upon discovering that she, like he, was twinless for the day, he'd insisted they pair up for the twin parade, even though the only thing their outfits had in common was that they were both wearing jeans. They'd had a great time putting together a silly costume consisting mostly of gym-towel capes and folded-newspaper hats.

But seeing Troy suddenly brought all her worries flooding back. How was she ever going to say good-bye to him?

He skidded to a stop in front of her. "Nice outfit," she told him, forcing a smile. "Very, um, dashing."

"Yeah, thanks." He grimaced and glanced down at himself, tugging at the hem of his glittery red jacket. "But never mind that—I really need to talk to you about something."

The expression on his face was so earnest and open that Gabriella felt like crying. This was ridiculous—she needed to tell him the truth about why she was acting so weird this week.

No, she thought firmly. It's bad enough that my Spirit Week is practically ruined. I can't ruin his, too. Or anybody else's, for that matter. I probably shouldn't even have told Kelsi; it was totally selfish of me to lay my bad news on her. But at least I swore her to secrecy so she won't tell anyone else and bum them out, too. I can tell them all the truth next week—that's soon enough.

"Gabriella?" Troy said. "Are you okay?"

Just then the PA system crackled to life. Principal Matsui came on, announcing that the twin parade was about to start.

"Come on!" Ryan exclaimed, adjusting his cape. "We need to get a spot near the front if we want to have any chance of winning this thing."

Gabriella shot Troy an apologetic glance. "Sorry, I have to go," she said. Grabbing Ryan by the hand, she took off with him toward the front of the parade.

# CHAPTER SIX

"Hold still, Gabriella. I need to pin this, and I don't want to poke you in the side."

Gabriella held her breath and stood as still as she could while her mother fiddled with the old-fashioned dress she was wearing. I think Mom is more enthusiastic about this Historical Character Day costume than I am, she thought, biting back a sigh.

"You didn't have to go to all this trouble," Gabriella said. "I'll just have a lab coat on over the dress, anyway."

"It's no problem." Her mother grabbed one of the pins she was holding in her mouth. "I want you to be the most accurate little Marie Curie you can be! Now keep still."

Gabriella smiled weakly and went back to holding her breath. She stared at the top of her mother's head, wishing she knew what thoughts were going on inside her brain. Was she thinking about the next big move? Trying to figure out how long it would take to find a new house in New York? Deciding when and how to break the news? Maybe she's doing the same thing I'm doing with my friends, Gabriella thought, waiting until after Spirit Week to deliver the blow.

Chewing her lower lip, Gabriella allowed her eyes to wander up and around her room, taking in the photos of her friends tucked into the mirror frame and the East High banner pinned to her bulletin board. This was the perfect time to ask her mother about that overheard phone conversation. But she just couldn't bear to do it right now. It was just too hard to think about leaving, especially this week, when everyone was so pumped up with school spirit. Knowing for sure that it was really happening would just be too much. If her mother confirmed that they were moving, Gabriella knew she would never be able to hide her feelings from her friends. And she was still determined not to ruin their Spirit Week with her bad news.

"There," her mother said, stepping back and brushing off her hands as she surveyed Gabriella's costume. "Now you look exactly like a turn-of-the-century Nobel prize–winning physicist." She laughed. "Maybe I need to start looking for a side job designing Broadway costumes or something!"

Gabriella gasped, feeling as if she'd just been punched in the stomach. Broadway costumes? Broadway was in New York City. Why would her mother mention Broadway right now? It seemed her earlier speculation might be true after all; her mother *did* have New York on her mind. . . .

"What's wrong?" Her mother immediately looked concerned.

"N-nothing," Gabriella stammered, doing her best to regain her composure. "I—uh—I just remembered I told Taylor I'd meet her before homeroom to help her with her outfit. I'm going to be late."

She yanked on her lab coat and rushed out of her room. She might as well accept the truth: she would be leaving again soon. All she could do was just try to enjoy whatever time she had left at East High.

Gabriella suddenly realized that the dance was only two days away. I'm going to ask Troy to the Spirit Ball today, she thought. No more distractions.

When she entered the school lobby a short while later, she looked around for Troy. Instead she spotted Sharpay and Ryan, who were dressed in what appeared to be authentic formal attire from the early twentieth century.

Sharpay spotted Gabriella, too. She hurried toward her, her long skirt rustling. "Let me guess—Madam Curie, right?" Sharpay said. "Cute. I played her in a musical once."

Ryan nodded. "Sharpay gave a fabulous performance. Very convincing."

"So who are you two supposed to be?" Gabriella asked, hoping it wasn't a rude question.

"I'm glad you asked." Sharpay raised her voice, glancing over at Principal Matsui, who happened to be passing by, as if hoping he would overhear. "We're dressed as Susannah and Jonathan Smith, the founders of East High."

"It wasn't my idea," Ryan put in with a shrug. "I was planning to come as Charlie Chaplin."

Sharpay shot him a slightly irritated glance. "That's right, it was *my* idea," she said, even more loudly. "Since this is supposed to be *Spirit* Week, I thought it would be nice to celebrate our school *spirit* by—hey!" she interrupted herself, jumping back as Chad and Jason almost crashed into her. They were racing through the school lobby, clowning around and tossing punches at each other. Both of them were dressed as Abraham Lincoln. "Watch it, you maniacs!" Sharpay cried. "This dress happens to be a very delicate historical artifact."

"Sorr-ry!" Chad said, giving Jason one last shove and then turning to stare at Sharpay and Ryan. He wrinkled his nose and sniffed. "It sure *smells* like a historical artifact."

Jason laughed. "Yeah—and all that historical dust is making me want to sneeze!"

"Hmmph!" Sharpay spun on her heels and turned up her nose.

Gabriella wasn't sure whether to laugh or roll her eyes. Before she could do either, she noticed Kelsi coming down the hall, struggling beneath the weight of a huge roll of red-and-black fabric.

"Hey! Careful with that." Gabriella rushed over and grabbed one end of the fabric roll.

"Thanks," Kelsi panted. "It *is* kind of heavy. But I really need to start taking stuff over to the gym. There's still a ton to do to get ready for tomorrow's pep rally. Zeke is supposed to be helping, but there was some kind of oven emergency, so . . ."

"Say no more," Gabriella said. "We'll all help you. Right, guys?" She glanced at Sharpay and Ryan.

"Are you kidding?" Sharpay cried. "Didn't you just hear me say that our costumes are historical artifacts? They're very fragile. We had to, like, sign papers before they'd let us rent them from the history museum."

"Hey, guys. What's going on?"

Gabriella turned to see Troy, dressed as Paul Revere, walking up to them. "Hi!" she said, blushing a little as she remembered why she'd been looking for him.

He smiled at her, then glanced at Kelsi. "Looks like you could use some help," he said, grabbing Gabriella's end of the fabric roll. "Where are we taking this?"

"Thanks, Troy," Kelsi said. "This way . . ."

Gabriella started to go along with them. This could be the perfect opportunity to ask Troy to the dance—as soon as they were out of the lobby, that is. She didn't mind asking him in front of Kelsi, but she wasn't crazy about doing it in front of Sharpay and Ryan, too.

But before she'd taken more than three steps, she felt someone grab her arm and yank her back. It was Sharpay.

"It's totally working!" Sharpay whispered, widening her eyes dramatically.

"What's working?" Gabriella asked. She glanced over her shoulder. Troy and Kelsi were already halfway down the hall.

Sharpay dropped her grip on Gabriella's arm and clasped her hands together. "Didn't you see the way Troy just smiled at you?" she exclaimed. "I can tell you've been playing it cool like I advised. He's definitely appreciating you more— it totally shows!"

"Huh?" Gabriella blinked, suddenly remembering their conversation the previous

Friday afternoon. "Oh—really?"

"Uh-huh." Sharpay smiled and winked broadly. "Keep up the good work, and you'll have him eating out of your hand. Toodles!" She waved and hurried off.

Gabriella turned to look for Troy and Kelsi, but they had already disappeared from sight around the corner of the hall. Gabriella was about to follow, but just then Principal Matsui came on the PA system, calling everyone to the lobby for the historical-costume parade.

"Rats," Gabriella muttered as kids started pouring into the lobby from all directions. She spotted Taylor coming in, dressed as Cleopatra. "I need to talk to you about something," Gabriella said, pulling her aside. She glanced around to make sure nobody else was listening. "It's about Troy."

"What about him?"

Gabriella noticed that Taylor didn't sound very interested. In fact, she was sort of scowling. But there were only a few moments before the parade started, so she continued on.

"You know I've been planning all week to ask him to the dance, right?" Gabriella said. "Well, remember how Sharpay told me I should play it cool, not seem too eager? I just saw her, and she thinks that's what I've been doing—and she thinks it's working! She says it's making Troy appreciate me more, or something. . . ." She took a deep breath. "So I guess what I'm asking is, do you think she could possibly be right?"

Taylor shrugged, her scowl deepening. "How should I know?" she snapped. "I'm the last person you should ask about guys. As far as I'm concerned, they all stink!"

"What?" Gabriella blinked in surprise. "Wait, I thought you and Chad made up on Twin Day."

"I thought so, too." Taylor tossed her head. "So then why did he still refuse to give me a straight answer about the dance when I asked him just now?"

She spun on her heels and marched into the classroom. Gabriella watched her go, feeling helpless. Why was it that the most complex chemistry equation was a piece of cake for her, yet she couldn't seem to figure out why anybody did anything?

# CHAPTER SEVEN

"Go Wildcats!" Troy whooped as he bounded into the gym with his teammates the next day. It was time for the lunchtime pep rally, and he couldn't wait! It was the perfect way to get the whole team psyched up for Saturday's game.

At least half the student body was already seated in the bleachers. They let out a cheer at Troy's entrance. Troy grinned and gave the entire gym a thumbs-up.

"This is going to be fun," Jason commented.

"Yeah," Chad agreed. "But why couldn't we have the pep rally during fourth period instead of lunch hour? I think I just failed that chemistry test."

"Don't think about that, man," another teammate advised. "Think about winning tomorrow!"

"Where's Zeke?" Jason asked as the guys made their way toward the section of bleachers reserved for them.

Chad shrugged, glancing around the gym. "Probably up to his elbows in cookie dough, the way he's been all week," he said. "I swear, the dude is making sure there will be at least a dozen cookies for every person at that dance."

Troy was still looking around, too, but not for Zeke. He was searching for Gabriella. But she was nowhere to be seen.

When they reached their seats, Sharpay was already sitting in the row of bleachers directly behind them. Sharpay waved at the team members. "Here come our little school heroes now," she cooed. "Ready for the game tomorrow, boys?"

Troy grinned as he took in her outfit. It was School Colors Day, and Sharpay was decked out in Wildcats red and black from head to toe—literally. She'd dyed her blond hair bright red. Her lips were a matching scarlet, and thick smudges of black eyeliner ringed her eyes. Her shirt was red, her pants glossy black, and her high-heeled black shoes had little red bows on them. At first Troy thought her bright red fingernails were smudged, but when he took a closer look, he saw that she'd painted tiny Wildcat logos on each nail.

"You're certainly showing your Wildcat spirit today, Sharpay," Troy commented, trying not to laugh.

"Is that what you call it?" Chad put in. "I would've guessed my dog just ate a box full of red and black crayons and then threw up on her." He grinned and traded high fives with Jason.

Sharpay smirked. "Very amusing—for a basketball Neanderthal, at least."

"So Sharpay, where's your brother?" Jason

asked. "I can't wait to see what *he's* wearing."

Sharpay shrugged. "He'll be here soon," she said. "Gabriella stopped him on the way in. Said she had something very important to ask him."

"Oh." Something about the way Sharpay turned to stare at him suddenly made Troy feel a little queasy. What was that all about?

Before he could think about it too much, Ryan appeared in the doorway. He strode toward them, ignoring the commotion going on around him. Like his sister, he was dressed all in red and black, though he'd left his hair color alone, settling for a jaunty red hat with a black feather. Troy was pretty sure it was the same one he'd borrowed on Twin Day.

"Hey Ryan, is Gabriella with you?" Troy asked when Ryan reached them. He craned his neck for a better look at the gym entrance, hoping to see her enter.

Ryan took a seat beside his sister and smoothed out the creases in his black pants. "She's on her way," he said. "I was just talking with her outside. Oh!" He turned to Sharpay, looking excited. "I also just saw Ms. Falstaff. She mentioned how much she's enjoyed our outfits all week."

Sharpay clapped her hands. "Excellent!" she said. "That's one more vote for me." She patted her bright red hair. "Not that I need it."

Chad rolled his eyes. "Be sure to let us know when you decide to run for national office, Sharpay."

"No thanks," Sharpay said. "I'll settle for East High Spirit Queen. At least for now." She leaned forward and touched Troy on the shoulder. "I'm really looking forward to it—especially to dancing with my king once we're crowned."

Troy grinned sheepishly as his teammates whooped and whistled. "Yeah, okay," he said. "Um, me, too, I guess. But I'm looking forward to dancing with my *own* date, too."

"Dude!" Jason clapped him on the back. "Does that mean Gabriella finally asked you?"

Troy felt more sheepish than ever. In fact, he

was pretty sure his cheeks were going as red as his Wildcats uniform. "Um, not exactly," he said. "Not yet, I mean. But I'm sure she will. Soon."

"Oh, really?" Sharpay stuck one hand out in front of herself, carefully studying her Wildcat fingernails. "I'm sure you're right, Troy. After all, there are still nearly thirty hours before the dance. And she *does* seem to be in an asking mood today—just ask my brother." She turned and winked at Ryan.

Ryan looked confused. "What do you mean, Sharpay?" hc said. "Gabriclla and I—"

"Don't need to tell everyone your business," Sharpay finished for him, hushing him with a finger to his lips.

Troy felt his heart stop. Was he going crazy, or was Sharpay implying that Gabriella had invited Ryan to be her date for the ball? Could that really be what she had wanted to ask him?

No way, he thought. Why would she ask *him*?

Then an image flashed into his mind, as vivid

as if he'd seen it yesterday—because he had. It was the image of Gabriella standing with Ryan in the lobby before homeroom. Oh, sure, Sharpay and Kelsi had been there, too. But that wasn't all. . . . There was the day before that, too, when he'd watched them run off together, hand in hand and laughing, dressed as twins. They certainly had seemed awfully chummy then. . . .

Before he could come out and ask Ryan what was going on, Principal Matsui and Coach Bolton walked into the gym, and the crowd let out a cheer. Troy turned around, staring out at the hectic pep-rally scene without really seeing any of it. This whole time, he'd thought about how humiliating it would be if Gabriella never asked him and he ended up without a date for the ball. But all along, he realized, he hadn't really believed it could happen. Not to him—not like this . . .

"Listen, Troy." Sharpay leaned forward, speaking directly into his ear. "I just want you to know, if you get tired of waiting around for a certain someone, my invitation still stands."

Troy gulped, glancing at her over his shoulder. . . .

". . . so I guess we should meet tomorrow afternoon to do all the last-minute decorating," Gabriella said, feeling distracted. She was standing in the hallway outside the gym with Zeke and Kelsi. A muffled cheer burst out from inside—it sounded as if the pep rally was starting. "Ryan just promised he'd come help out and ask Sharpay to come, too, so if we can get a few more people . . ."

"Cool," Zeke said, looking equally distracted. "Thanks for helping out. Come on, we'd better get in there."

The three of them raced down the hall toward the gym. Gabriella couldn't believe the day was already half over and she still hadn't asked Troy to the dance. Despite her determination, she'd never found another chance alone with him the day before. And he'd had to run off right after classes ended for an extra basketball practice.

I really should have called him last night after dinner, she thought.

But that hadn't quite happened, either. First she'd spent half an hour on the phone with Taylor, trying to convince her that she should give Chad another chance instead of staying home to do her chemistry homework on Saturday night. Then Kelsi called to see how she was holding up, and the two of them had spent another half an hour on the phone.

Once Gabriella had hung up, her mother finally arrived home from work, looking ragged and exhausted. That had made Gabriella feel even more distracted by the whole moving situation, and by the time she remembered the dance it was too late to call Troy.

Oh, well, she thought, biting her lip. Troy's got to assume we're going together, right? Asking him is just a formality—even though it *feels* way scarier than that!

The gym was a madhouse when they entered.

Principal Matsui was standing on the center line with Coach Bolton, trying to adjust the microphone in front of them. The cheerleaders were nearby, bouncing around, doing one of their routines, and most of the students were clapping and hollering along.

Gabriella followed Zeke as he loped over toward the team bench. She smiled when she spotted Troy among the others. Most of his teammates were jumping around or watching the cheerleaders, but he was still seated, twisting around to talk to someone behind him. When she got a little closer, Gabriella saw that he was talking with Sharpay.

Pushing her way past the excited cheerleaders, Gabriella finally reached the team bench. She took a deep breath, not wanting to miss yet another opportunity. Her heart was pounding, but she did her best to ignore that.

This only *seems* scary, she reminded herself. It'll probably be sort of like that first duet Troy and I ever sang together—at first I thought I was going to throw up or at least faint. But once I got started, it was actually fun.

"Troy!" she blurted out, clambering over the bleacher seat. "I need to ask you something. Actually, it's something I've been meaning to ask you all week . . ."

"Huh?" he shouted over the noise of the crowd. Principal Matsui's microphone had just let out a loud whine of feedback, and most of the students were howling and stomping their feet on the bleachers in response. "I can't hear you!"

Gabriella cleared her throat and leaned closer. "I want to ask you something!" she cried. "Will you go to the Spirit Ball with me?"

She smiled, letting out a huge sigh of relief. Her guess had been right—once the words were out, it suddenly didn't seem so scary after all.

Then she noticed Troy's face. He was wearing an expression of shock and confusion. Her smile faded. "What's wrong?" she asked.

Sharpay leaned forward. "Sorry, Gabriella," she said with a smirk. "You're a little late to the party. See, Troy just agreed to go to the dance with me."

# CHAPTER EIGHT

"All right, people, settle down." Ms. Darbus clapped her hands for attention. "In case you've forgotten, this is still an institution of learning. And this is drama class, *not* how-to-behave-like-jungle-creatures class."

"Yo, how can we think about boring old drama stuff when we have a game to win tomorrow?" Chad cried, pumping his fist in the air. Several of the other students laughed and cheered.

Gabriella smiled along weakly. But she wasn't

in the mood for cheering. She was still stunned about Troy and Sharpay. Unfortunately, the pep rally had started right after Sharpay's announcement, so Gabriella hadn't been able to talk to Troy about it.

How could he do this? she wondered, glancing over her shoulder at him. To her surprise, he was staring back at her somberly. Feeling her cheeks go pink, she quickly ducked her head and pretended to be very busy pulling her drama class notebook out of her bag.

When she looked up again, Ms. Darbus was glaring at Chad. "All right, Mr. Danforth," she said icily. "If you find my class so dull, perhaps a pop quiz on *The Taming of the Shrew* will get your attention, hmm?" She rolled the *r* in "shrew" dramatically.

The entire class groaned. "No way, Ms. D!" Zeke exclaimed. "We can't have a pop quiz during Spirit Week. It's just not—well—*spirited*!"

The drama teacher crossed her arms over the

front of her flowing purple tunic. "That's *exactly* why we're having one," she said. "This whole school has become entirely too focused on tomorrow's silly sports contest. Pencils out, please, and eyes on your own paper . . ."

Soon the classroom was silent as the students pored over their quizzes. Gabriella was usually one of the first ones finished with any quiz, but today she was having trouble focusing on the paper in front of her.

Like it's not bad enough that I'll be moving away soon, she thought, staring at a question on the quiz without really seeing it. Now I won't even get to enjoy my one and only Spirit Ball at East High.

She sighed, doodling a little Wildcat *W* in the margin of her paper. So much for the dance being her last big hurrah. If she wasn't going with Troy, she wasn't sure there was any point in going at all. . . .

*"Wildcats, in the house!"*

Gabriella jumped, along with the rest of the

class, as Sharpay suddenly leaped out of her seat and burst into a full-throated rendition of the school fight song. Ms. Darbus was so startled that she nearly fell off her thronelike chair at the front of the room.

"Ms. Evans!" she snapped, grasping the arms of her chair. "What is the meaning of this outburst?"

"Sorry, Ms. Darbus," Sharpay said, not sounding sorry at all. "I guess I just got overwhelmed with school spirit for a minute there. You know—*Wildcats, in the house! Everybody say it now . . .*" Soon she was singing again.

Ms. Darbus waved her hands in the air helplessly for several seconds before finally sputtering out, "Silence!"

Sharpay paused in her song. "Oh, was I doing it again?" she said sweetly. "I really just can't seem to control myself."

By now most of the class was snickering. Gabriella rolled her eyes. Even in the distracted mood she'd been in all week, it had been impossible not to notice that Sharpay was campaigning hard for that Spirit Queen title.

That's probably why she wanted to go to the dance with Troy, she thought. He's sure to be named Spirit King, and if there's one thing Sharpay adores it's a nice, neat, happy Broadway ending.

"I suggest you figure out how to control yourself, Ms. Evans—immediately," Ms. Darbus said, glaring at Sharpay. "Otherwise, you'll be able to sing to your heart's content in a special Saturday-night detention session tomorrow."

Sharpay immediately snapped her mouth shut and sat down. "Sorry," she said. "Won't happen again."

The rest of the class seemed to inch by at glacial speed. But finally the bell rang, releasing them. Gabriella gathered up her things quickly. She was pretty sure she'd flubbed that quiz, but she had bigger things on her mind. She needed to talk to Troy and find out why he'd agreed to go to the ball with Sharpay.

But she'd barely taken three steps out of the room when Zeke caught up with her. "Gabriella!" he panted, looking slightly panicky. "Can you help me? I need to carry a whole bunch of cookies down to the storage room before basketball practice starts."

Gabriella hesitated for only a split second. Then she nodded. "Okay," she said, "lead the way."

Moments later they were tucking the cookies safely into big coolers in the storage room off the gym. Halfway back to the kitchen, Kelsi appeared in the doorway of the auditorium, looking panicked.

"Do either of you have a spare second?" she asked. "We're trying to get the last few garlands woven so we can hang them up tomorrow, and we still need to paint that Wildcat cutout, but there are only four of us today, and . . ."

Gabriella glanced at Zeke, hoping he'd volunteer. Then she remembered that he had to rush off for basketball practice.

"I'll help," she said. "Just show me what to do."

For the next hour or two, Kelsi and the rest of the decorations committee kept Gabriella busy weaving, painting, and just generally helping out. When Zeke finally dashed back in, still dressed in his uniform, he looked delighted at their progress. "Gabriella, you're an angel for helping," Zeke told her. "I'll make sure you get all the cookies you can eat at the ball tomorrow night. Maybe I'll even make you a crème brûlée!"

"Thanks," Gabriella said with a smile. "But it's no problem, really. Besides, I'm not sure I'm even going to the ball."

"What?" Kelsi squeaked, looking shocked. "But you have to go! This isn't because of—um, *you* know—is it?" She bit her lip and shot a glance at Zeke.

Realizing she was referring to the moving secret, Gabriella quickly shook her head, not wanting Zeke to catch on. "I was planning to go," she said, "but since I don't have a date . . ."

"That's okay," Zeke said quickly. "I don't have a date, either. I've been too busy baking and helping with the decorating stuff to even think about that sort of thing." He shrugged. "No big deal. Lots of people go stag."

"Yeah," Kelsi added. "I don't have a date, either. Maybe the three of us can go and hang out together?"

Gabriella hesitated. Both of them were staring at her with beseeching looks on their faces.

How can I say no? she thought. Especially after all the hard work they've put into this dance . . .

"Well . . . okay," she said at last. "That sounds like fun. It's a date." She laughed and rolled her eyes. "Or a nondate. Or whatever."

"Cool." Zeke smiled. "Now if you'll excuse me, my macaroons should be ready by now. . . ."

By the time Gabriella made her escape, the school hallways were almost deserted. As she hurried toward the gym, she spotted a pair of guys from the team wandering along with towels slung over their shoulders.

"Hey!" she called to them. "Did everybody leave practice already?"

"Uh-huh," one of the guys replied. "Like half an hour ago."

The other player nodded. "Coach wants us to go home and rest up for the big game."

"Oh." Gabriella slumped against the nearest row of lockers. "Um, good luck tomorrow."

So she was too late. No, she reminded herself, I was too late a couple of hours ago at that pep rally. Why make a big deal over it now? Troy and I can talk things out next week—*if* it still matters after everyone hears my other news.


"Yo, what's wrong with you, Troy?" Chad exclaimed. "That's the sixth free throw you've missed in a row!"

"Yeah," Jason added. He was sitting on the gym floor nearby watching Troy and Chad goof off after practice. The coach and the rest of the team had left a while ago, but the three of them were hanging out, waiting for Zeke to return from the kitchen. "You'd better play better than that tomorrow, or we're going to get slaughtered out there."

Troy sighed and jogged in to grab the rebound. "I know," he said. "I guess I just have a lot on my mind."

That was an understatement. He couldn't seem to stop thinking about the expression on Gabriella's face when she'd heard that he and Sharpay were going to the dance together. How could he have been so stupid? This whole time he'd been afraid that she didn't want to go with him. And now she thought *he* didn't want to go with *her*, when nothing could be farther from the truth!

"Well, pull it together, man," Jason said. "The Spirit Ball isn't going to be much fun if we blow the big game tomorrow."

"I guess." Troy shrugged. "Actually, I was sort of thinking I might not go to the ball."

"What?" Chad's eyes widened. "What are you talking about? You have to go—you're going to be the Spirit King!"

Jason nodded, jumping to his feet and hurrying over to grab the ball out of Troy's hands. "Yeah, don't talk crazy, Troy!" he exclaimed. "You have to be there to witness my hot date with Ami the cheerleader."

Chad gave Jason a shove. "Give it up, man. You know you were her second choice." But his heart didn't seem to be in the teasing. He shot Troy a worried glance. "You're just kidding around about this, right? You wouldn't really skip the dance?"

Troy hesitated. His friends looked so worried and disappointed that he couldn't stand it. The last thing he wanted to do was mess things up further by bumming out his teammates so they wouldn't play their best tomorrow.

"Sure, I was just joking around," he said. "Of course I'll go."

They laughed, looking relieved, and Troy forced a smile. I'll go, he thought. I just won't expect to have a good time.

# CHAPTER NINE

*B*ZZZZZT!

The final buzzer went off, ending the big game. The East High gymnasium erupted into wild cheers. "We did it!" the cheerleaders howled, pom-poms flashing as they leaped onto the court. "Wildcats, in the house!"

Troy grinned, glancing up at the scoreboard. HOME: 62, VISITORS: 54.

"Way to go, captain!" Chad shouted, hurling himself at Troy and pounding him on the back. "Glad you got your groove back."

"Yeah, man. After yesterday, I was worried!" Jason joined them, jumping up and down and pumping his fist.

Troy spotted Zeke jogging toward them and raised both hands for a double high five. "Check it out, guys—here's our MVP," he said. The score had been tied for most of the game until Zeke had made a big play, sinking two three-pointers in a row. After that the momentum had changed, and it was all Wildcats.

Zeke grinned. "Thanks. But this win was a team effort—like always!"

Troy glanced at the stands, which were overflowing with excited Wildcats fans. Even so, he quickly picked out Gabriella. She was sitting with Taylor a few rows behind the team bench.

She saw him looking and waved, while Taylor shot him a thumbs-up. Troy waved back, glad that the whole Spirit Ball–date fiasco hadn't kept Gabriella away from the game. He wished he could have talked to her about the whole dance mess, but after basketball practice yesterday his father had insisted on taking the whole family out for a pregame dinner. By the time they got home it had been too late to call.

His smile faded as he noticed Sharpay sitting nearby. She was waving a huge sign that read GO WILDCATS! When she saw Troy looking, she jumped up and waved. Then she flipped her sign over. On the other side, in bright Wildcat red, were the words TROY RULES! Below that was a little drawing. Troy squinted at it, feeling his face turn red as he realized it was a picture of himself and Sharpay standing hand in hand. As if that weren't bad enough, both of them were wearing little gold crowns.

Troy shuddered. He had nothing against Sharpay, but he definitely wasn't looking forward to going to the dance with her. Especially when he really *should* be going with someone else . . .

"Come on, dude," Chad said, slapping him on

the back and breaking him out of his thoughts. "Let's hit the showers. We need to get out of here and get ready for the dance."

Troy smiled weakly. A promise was a promise. . . . "You're on," he said. "So does this mean you and Taylor are back together again?"

"Sort of," Chad said. "Um, I guess. That is, I haven't really asked her." He shrugged. "But hey, I'm sure things will work out."

Troy couldn't help feeling a twinge of envy. How could Chad be so casual about something like that? But he pushed the thought aside. "Let's go," Troy said, leading the way toward the locker room.

Gabriella stared at herself in the full-length mirror on the bathroom door, smoothing her skirt. She was dressed in a pretty blue dress with a flowing skirt. Her dark hair was piled loosely atop her head, allowing a few tendrils to fall in soft curls around her face. The only thing wrong with the picture was her expression. No matter what she did, she couldn't seem to muster a smile.

"Oh, honey! You look beautiful!"

Gabriella turned to see her mother standing in the hallway, her hands clasped in front of her and a proud smile on her face. For once, her mother had been home all day, though she'd been working at the computer for most of the time Gabriella had spent getting ready.

"Thanks." Gabriella tried to sound chipper but failed miserably. Her voice came out in a sad croak.

Her mother immediately noticed her lack of enthusiasm. Her smile was replaced by a look of concern. "What's wrong?" she asked. "Aren't you feeling well?" She hurried forward to put a hand to Gabriella's forehead.

Gabriella brushed her away. "It's nothing like that," she mumbled, feeling tears spring to her eyes. This whole time she'd been planning to wait until after Spirit Week to confront her mother about what she'd overheard—to face the truth. But suddenly she just couldn't stand it for another second. "I'm just upset because this could be my last dance ever at East High!"

Her mother looked confused. "What are you talking about?" she asked. "There will be lots of other dances."

"But not for me, right? Not here." Gabriella shook her head, trying desperately to contain her tears. "You don't have to keep it a secret anymore, Mom. I heard you on the phone the other night. I know we're moving again."

"What?" This time her mother looked startled. "Moving? Where did you get that idea?"

"From you." Gabriella quickly told her about the phone call she'd overheard. "Sorry for eavesdropping—I didn't mean to. But I couldn't help it and then when I heard what you were talking about I—"

"Wait!" Her mother held up one hand. "You mean you heard me talking about going to New York and thought we were *moving* there?" She laughed and put both hands to her cheeks.

Gabriella stared at her. "Why are you laughing? This isn't funny."

"I'm sorry, honey." Her mother swallowed another chuckle. "I don't mean to laugh; I can see that you're upset. But there's no reason to be—we're not going anywhere. It's just like I told you on your first day at East High. We're here until you graduate."

"But . . . but . . ." Gabriella blinked, trying to take in what her mother was saying. "Then why were you talking about notifying my school before you go to New York? And then a couple of days ago you were joking about designing Broadway outfits on the side, and so I just thought . . ."

Her mother stepped forward and put an arm around Gabriella's shoulders, giving her a hug. "I'm taking a business trip to New York City in a month or two," she explained. "And since I'll have a few free days while I'm there, I thought it would be fun if you came along." She smiled. "And it's true, I might have had Broadway on my mind lately—with your new interest in musical theater, I thought we could try to see a couple of shows while we're there."

Gabriella just stared at her. Could it be true? "But you've been working so hard lately," she said. "All those late hours . . ."

"You're right, I have, and I'm sorry I haven't had more time to spend with you." Her mother shrugged. "I thought I told you, though—my company is in the middle of switching over to a new computer system."

Now that she mentioned it, that did sound vaguely familiar to Gabriella. But she still wasn't sure what it had to do with anything. "Um, so?"

"So we're all having to do twice as much work as usual just to keep up." Her mother gave her shoulders an extra squeeze. "That's why I told my boss I couldn't possibly do the New York trip until all that's settled."

"Oh." The pieces were falling into place. Now that she knew the truth, Gabriella was starting to feel kind of stupid. How could she have jumped to conclusions without taking a more careful look at all the facts? If she did that sort of thing in chemistry class, she would fail—if she didn't blow up the lab first.

Her mother smiled and stepped back, reaching out to adjust a strand of hair falling down into Gabriella's eyes. "So, are you ready to go enjoy your dance now?" she asked.

"Sure!" Gabriella smiled—and this time it took no effort at all. It felt as if a huge weight had been lifted off her shoulders. She couldn't wait to tell Kelsi the good news. Of course, she still wasn't sure what was going on with Troy. . . .

But we'll work it out, she thought with a shiver of relief. After all, we have plenty of time.

# CHAPTER TEN

"Smile, Troy. Everybody's looking at us." Sharpay patted her blond hair, which was twisted up on top of her head in an elaborate style. "Of course, can you blame them? We look sensational. Talk about a power couple!"

Troy forced a weak smile. He was used to people staring at him when he played ball, but it definitely felt strange to walk into the dance with Sharpay clinging to his arm. His heart was thumping beneath his dark blazer, and his palms felt sweaty.

What's my problem? he wondered. I've only walked into this gym a thousand times before.

But tonight felt different. Much different. And it was only partly because the East High gym didn't look anything like itself. The decorations committee had done a fantastic job, transforming it completely in the few hours since the game had finished. It was still decked out in Wildcat colors, but instead of team banners and retired jerseys, those colors came from balloons, painted backdrops, and garlands of streamers. The place was already packed.

"Hey, Bolton! Nice shooting today!" somebody called from nearby.

Troy raised a hand in response, but Sharpay answered before he could say anything. "Thank you, anonymous person," she called out. "Troy always enjoys comments from his fans."

"Knock it off, Sharpay," Troy muttered. "You're making me sound like a snob."

She raised one carefully groomed eyebrow.

"Isn't that sweet," she said. "Our little superstar is a populist at heart." She shrugged. "You'll get over that after a while in the spotlight. Trust me."

Troy barely heard her. He'd glanced over his shoulder just in time to see Gabriella walking into the gym with Kelsi and Zeke. The three of them were all holding hands and giggling.

Troy's heart almost stopped. He had never seen Gabriella look quite so beautiful. As he watched, she threw her head back and laughed at something Zeke had just said, looking happy and excited. Then she waved to Taylor, who was hurrying toward her.

"Excuse me," Troy said to Sharpay. "I just need to go say hi to—"

But Sharpay had followed his gaze and spotted Gabriella herself. "Not so fast," she interrupted, yanking him back before he could get more than two steps away. "You're my date, remember? All mine." She smiled smugly. "That means you'd better stay put. Especially since it's almost time for Principal Matsui to crown the Spirit King and Queen."

"Oh, my gosh, you guys! The gym looks amazing!" Taylor exclaimed.

Gabriella smiled and glanced at Kelsi and Zeke. "Thanks," they all said in unison.

Taylor wrinkled her nose. "Too bad you couldn't do anything about the *smell*."

Gabriella was about to answer that she didn't smell anything, but then she saw that Taylor was scowling at Chad, who was jogging toward them. He looked cute in a red tie and a coat that was a little too big for him. He traded an elaborate high-five greeting with Zeke, then turned to face Taylor.

"Hello," Taylor said, her voice cool. "Do I know you?"

"Look," Chad said, taking a step toward her. "Don't be like that, okay?"

Zeke rolled his eyes. "Later, dude," he said. "I'd better go check on the cookies."

Chad was still staring at Taylor. "I already said I was sorry for goofing with you at the mall."

"Yeah." Taylor crossed her arms. "Easy to say that without all your friends watching."

Chad raised an eyebrow. "Is that what you're worried about?" he said. "You think I'm, like, embarrassed to be seen with you or something?"

"Maybe." Taylor shrugged. "Are you saying that's not it?"

"Maybe," Chad said.

Gabriella winced and exchanged a glance with Kelsi. Wrong thing to say, she thought. She could tell Chad was just joking around, as usual. But she could also tell that Taylor wasn't amused this time.

Taylor was glaring at Chad. "Then *maybe* you don't really want to be here with me after all," she said. She turned and started to walk away, chin in the air.

"Wait!" Chad sounded worried as he raced after her. "Hold on a second, okay? I was just goofing around, that's all. That's why I didn't say yes right away, too. I do want to be here with you—really! I swear!"

Taylor glanced over her shoulder at him. "Actions speak louder than words, Chad. Even *your* words—and they're pretty loud."

"Oh, yeah? Well, you just gave me the perfect idea about how to prove it to you." Chad cleared his throat, then grabbed Taylor's hand and held it up in the air. "Listen up, everyone!" he bellowed at the top of his lungs. "See this girl here? Me and her are here *together*, got that? And I'm proud of it! Hear me? *Proud, I say!*"

Gabriella giggled at the startled look on Taylor's face. People had turned to stare at them from all around, and a gaggle of cheerleaders standing nearby bent toward one another to whisper and laugh. Even Zeke had stopped halfway to the refreshments table to look back in shock.

Taylor's look of surprise was already turning to one of amusement. "Oh, Chad." She giggled. "You're such a weirdo. But I *might* forgive you if you get me a glass of punch."

Gabriella exchanged a smile with Kelsi as Taylor and Chad walked off together. She was glad to see that the two of them were back on track. Now if she could just straighten things out with Troy . . .

Before she could look for him, Principal Matsui stepped up onto a little platform beneath the home team basket and turned on his microphone. A whine of feedback got everyone's attention.

"Oh, good," Gabriella said. "He must be getting ready to announce the Spirit King and Queen. This should be fun."

Kelsi rolled her eyes. "Ooh, the suspense," she said sarcastically. "Everyone knows Troy and Sharpay are going to win."

"As you all know, the faculty and I have been watching you carefully all week to see which boy and girl we think showed the most school spirit during Spirit Week," Principal Matsui said. "I'm going to name our six finalists. Two of them will be our king and queen, and the others will serve as their royal court. I'll call the finalists first in alphabetical order. Please come up here if your name is called." He cleared his throat and shuffled his notes. "Zeke Baylor!"

"Way to go, Zeke!" Chad howled, cupping both hands around his mouth.

Kelsi clapped. "That's so cool!" she cried. "You know, I never knew Zeke very well before. But he really does have a lot of school spirit."

"True," Gabriella said. "Plus he made that awesome play in the game today."

"Next," Principal Matsui continued, "I'd like to see Troy Bolton."

This time everyone cheered. Gabriella craned her neck to get a better look as Troy made his way toward the principal. He was grinning bashfully and looking handsome in his coat and tie.

"Now, can I see Ryan Evans?" Principal Matsui called next. "And Sharpay Evans."

"He might as well stop right there," Kelsi said, clapping politely along with everyone else.

"Oh, come on," Gabriella said with a laugh. "Don't try to cheat a couple of cheerleaders out of their big mo—"

"Gabriella Montez," Principal Matsui called.

"What?" Gabriella squeaked, startled.

"Go up there!" Kelsi said, grinning and giving her a shove.

"And Kelsi Nielsen," the principal finished. "Come on up!"

This time Gabriella was the one to grin. She grabbed Kelsi by the hand. "Come on," she said. "Our royal subjects await."

She couldn't help feeling bashful as she dragged Kelsi forward. It still felt kind of strange to know that all eyes were on her. But starring in the winter musical had helped her get over some of her stage fright. She even managed to wave a little as she made her way through the crowd to take her place with the others.

"Congrats," Troy whispered, leaning closer to her and smiling.

"You, too," she said, suddenly feeling shy.

"Listen, Troy. I'm sorry I didn't—"

"Don't worry about it," he whispered back. "I'm sorry I—you know." He tilted his head toward Sharpay. "I'll explain later."

"Me, too." Gabriella smiled at him, knowing without a doubt that things would be back to normal between them very soon. "As soon as this king-and-queen thing is over, we can talk."

"Hush!" Sharpay hissed at both of them. "He's about to announce my—I mean, announce the winners' names."

Sure enough, Principal Matsui was shuffling his papers again. "Without further ado," he said into the microphone, "I give you your Spirit King and Queen—Zeke Baylor and Kelsi Nielsen!"

"What?" Zeke exclaimed, looking surprised.

"What?" Kelsi cried, looking stunned.

"What?" Sharpay squawked loudly, looking horrified. "You're kidding, right? Her? But she's—she's . . ." She seemed to run out of words as she stared at Kelsi. "She's not even wearing

Wildcat colors!" she sputtered at last, pointing dramatically at Kelsi's green dress.

Principal Matsui looked confused. "I'm sorry, Sharpay," he said. "That really wasn't a requirement."

"Ooh!" This time Sharpay didn't even try. Throwing both hands over her head, she stomped off.

"Sharpay, wait!" Ryan called, charging off after her.

The principal shrugged, then spoke into the microphone again. "Congratulations to Zeke and Kelsi," he said. "Both of them showed true school spirit by working tirelessly this week to make this dance happen. So let's see them enjoy it—get out there and dance, you two!"

Zeke had recovered from his surprise by now and appeared to be enjoying himself as he waved to the crowd. Then he turned to Kelsi, who still hadn't moved.

"May I, Your Majesty?" he said, holding out a hand as the DJ started a song.

"Go on!" Gabriella whispered with a grin, shoving Kelsi toward him.

A moment later, the two of them were swaying awkwardly to the music. Zeke kept looking around and grinning uncertainly, while Kelsi kept her eyes on her own feet.

"They don't look too happy to be out there dancing in front of everyone, do they?" Troy commented to Gabriella.

"Not really." She shot him a sidelong glance. "Maybe we should get out there and help them out?"

He grinned and took her by the hand. "I thought you'd never ask."

Something new is on the way!
Look for the next book in the Disney High
School Musical: Stories from East High series. . .

# POETRY
# IN MOTION

By Alice Alfonsi

Based on the Disney Channel Original Movie
"High School Musical", written by Peter Barsocchini

Troy Bolton stifled a yawn. At the front of the room, Ms. Barrington was reading yet another Scottish ode.

English was Troy's first class after lunch. Today he'd downed two cartons of milk and a turkey sandwich—good choices for athletic nutrition, but a seriously bad combo for listening to two-hundred-year-old poetry. Pinching the back of his hand, Troy tried to stay alert. But his eyelids felt as if they'd been loaded down with free weights. His head dropped once, twice, three times. Then *bop!* A little paper airplane hit him. Troy sat straight up. He was definitely awake now.

The tiny projectile had dropped onto his desk. He picked it up and unfolded the paper. Right away, he recognized the neat, delicate hand-writing. . . .

*O stay awake, Troy Bolton!*
*Push your comprehension.*
*'Cause if you nod off one more time,*
*you'll be napping in detention!*
                    *Poetically yours,*
                    *Gabriella*

Before he could stop himself, Troy laughed out loud.

At the front of the room, the teacher looked up from her textbook. "Is something *funny*, Mr. Bolton?"

"No, Ms. Barrington," Troy said. He quickly crumpled the note, hiding it in his fist.

The tall, slender teacher peered at him through her black oval-shaped glasses. Ms. Barrington wasn't very old, but her floor-length skirts, severely upswept red hair, and love of eighteenth-century poetry made her seem ancient to Troy.

"It certainly *sounds* as though you found something amusing in Robert Burns' poem," she said. "Why don't you share it with us?"

Troy silently groaned. Gabriella Montez was sitting in the next row. She'd been smiling at him when he read her funny note. Now that it had triggered trouble, she looked really upset.

Sorry, she silently mouthed to Troy.

It's okay, he mouthed back.

Ms. Barrington tapped her foot. "Mr. Bolton? I'm waiting." She glanced at Gabriella and narrowed her eyes. "Enlighten us all with your reaction to this poet's words. What exactly made you laugh?"

"Umm . . ." Troy swallowed. He felt heat rising in his cheeks.

Gabriella was about to speak up when a voice came from across the room.

"My man wasn't laughing," Chad Danforth insisted.

Ms. Barrington put a hand on her hip and turned her head. Now she had a new target. "Is that right, Mr. Danforth?"

Troy froze. Chad was one of his best friends. He always watched Troy's back, especially on the basketball court. But now was not the time for his teammate to execute a fake out!

"Straight up," Chad said. "You misheard Troy. He was just clearing his throat."

Ms. Barrington narrowed her gaze. "I misheard him?"

"Sure," Chad said. "I mean, what dude in his right mind would laugh at what you just read?"

Troy cringed. "Uh, right. Sorry to interrupt, Ms. Barrington. I just had to, you know, clear my dry throat. Like Chad said."

"You see how powerful that poem was?" Chad went on. "Like subliminal advertising or something."

"All right, Chad. That's enough." Ms. Barrington cleared her own throat. "Let's move on, shall we?"

"Okay by me," Chad mumbled, exchanging a glance with his teammates in the last row. Two points, he silently mouthed to them.

Zeke Baylor and Jason Cross quietly sniggered, and Troy exhaled with relief. He had no doubt that Chad had just saved him and Gabriella from all the joys of detention.

At the front of the room, Ms. Barrington lifted her chin and addressed the class. "For the last four weeks, you've all been studying a number of poets. Now it's time to test what you've absorbed."

She snapped her textbook shut and leaned back against the edge of her desk. "But I'm not going to give you a traditional multiple-choice quiz. In my view, that's not the way to test whether you've really learned what poetry is all about. Next Tuesday, at a special school assembly, each of you will read an original poem. This assignment will be a very important part of your semester grade. But I'm sure each of you will rise to the occasion."

Chad scratched his head of floppy brown hair. "Excuse me, Ms. Barrington?" He waved his hand. "What do you mean, each of us will 'read an original poem'?"

The English teacher frowned. "What's not to understand, Chad? You will write a poem. Then you will read the poem you wrote. Simple."

"But . . ." Chad blinked. "In front of the whole school?"

"Yes, in front of the whole school. As I said, it's a very special assembly." Mrs. Barrington clapped her hands.

"So, will you accept poems written in any style?" Taylor asked, turning to a fresh page in her notebook. "Or just the Romantic style?" She lifted her pen, ready to scribble a detailed answer.

"Any style of poetry is welcome," Ms. Barrington said. "We've covered a number of them in class, but I've given you all a reading list. Inspiration abounds! Take advantage of it."

Kelsi's hand went up again. She nervously pushed up her round glasses. "Ms. Barrington?" she asked, her small voice barely rising above the brim of her cap. "You're not really going to make it mandatory that we read our own poems, are you?"

"Of course!" Ms. Barrington boomed. "Reading your own poetry is a vital experience and an essential part of the assignment."

Now Sharpay Evans raised her hand. "I, for one, think it's a brilliant assignment! Thank you, Ms. Barrington, for giving us this opportunity to spotlight our individual talents!"

Ms. Barrington nodded. "You're welcome, Sharpay."

Troy noticed Taylor rolling her eyes. Gabriella just sighed. Then the bell rang, and everyone scattered.

"Dude, I owe you," Troy said, walking up to Chad a few minutes later. "Thanks for the save back there."

"No problem." Chad said. "Just pay me back with some sweet passes on the court."

"You got it," Troy smiled, and the two sealed the deal by knocking fists.

Taylor McKessie tossed Chad a warm smile as she walked into the hallway. "Easy assignment, huh, Chad?" she called.

"The assignment?" Chad said, automatically tensing. "Uh . . . sure . . . piece o' cake," he told her, forcing a smile and trying to seem relaxed.

The moment Taylor was gone, he grimaced. "As if I'm going to do it," he whispered to Troy. "Yeah, right."

Troy blinked. "What do you mean?"

"I'm not doing that poetry assignment," Chad said. "That's what I mean."

Troy couldn't believe what he was hearing. "Chad, you have to. You heard Ms. Barrington. It's a big part of your semester grade."

Chad waved his hand. "I'll tell her I've got writer's block or something. She'll let me off the hook. But I am *not* getting up on East's auditorium stage, in front of the entire school, spouting rhymes about rainbows and red, red, roses. This whole poetry thing freaks me out!"

"Freaks you out?" Sharpay piped up, overhearing him. She tossed her blond hair and threw a special grin Troy's way. "What's the biggie, guys? Roses are red, violets are blue. The *writing* is simple. What's key is the *presentation*. Just find the right costume, practice in front of a mirror, and you'll do fine!"

Chad looked horrified.

Sharpay didn't notice. She checked her watch. "Sorry, I've got to run," she chirped, dashing off. "Drama class next, and I haven't warmed my vocal chords! Buh-bye!"

Chad shuddered. He turned to Troy. "Did you hear what she said?" he whispered. "A *costume*?"

"Oh, wow. That's right. I forgot." Troy

smacked his forehead, suddenly remembering. "Your leotard incident."

"Dude, don't even go there." Chad shook his head, looking a little sick to his stomach. He glanced around, making sure no one was close enough to hear.

Troy didn't blame him. When they were in fourth grade, their teacher had convinced Chad to recite a poem at the Albuquerque Renaissance Fair. Unfortunately, she'd failed to warn him that he'd have to wear Elizabethan tights, silk bloomers, and a hat with a feather.

All the boys in their class were laughing hysterically at him the second he stepped onto the stage. Chad had memorized the love poem perfectly. He was actually hoping to impress a girl named Rhonda. But when he saw every boy in his class laughing in the front row, he forgot the lines and began to stammer. Then he dropped his hat, bent over to pick it up, and his bloomers split open.

It wasn't a good day.

Six months later, Rhonda moved to Denver. But Chad never forgot the look on her face as he ran off the stage, mortified.

"I can't do it, man," Chad whispered. "I just can't."

"But—"

"Sorry." Chad shook his head. "I'll catch you later!"

Troy stood like a statue in the hallway. A couple of kids bumped into him. He didn't notice. He was too upset by what Chad intended to do—and not do.

Troy doubted very much that Ms. Barrington was going to let anyone off the hook for this assignment. Their English teacher was really tough. She'd never accept an excuse of "writer's block."